PUFFIN BOOK

ADDY THE BADDY AND THE BABY

Margaret Joy was born on Tyneside, and has lived in Bristol, on Teesside, and in other parts of the British Isles. She started writing children's stories for radio and television when her own children were young. After teaching for some years, she continued writing and has published over twenty books. She and her husband are now settled in North Wales, where she enjoys living and writing in beautiful surroundings.

Some other books by Margaret Joy

ADDY THE BADDY
LATE KICK-OFF
SEE YOU AT THE MATCH

Margaret Joy
Addy the Baddy
and the Baby

Illustrated by Ann Kronheimer

PUFFIN BOOKS

For Bridget, Isabel,
Tom and Gerard, Paul and Clare

PUFFIN BOOKS

Published by the Penguin Group
Penguin Books Ltd, 27 Wrights Lane, London W8 5TZ, England
Penguin Putnam Inc., 375 Hudson Street, New York, New York 10014, USA
Penguin Books Australia Ltd, Ringwood, Victoria, Australia
Penguin Books Canada Ltd, 10 Alcorn Avenue, Toronto, Ontario, Canada M4V 3B2
Penguin Books (NZ) Ltd, Private Bag 102902, NSMC, Auckland, New Zealand

Penguin Books Ltd, Registered Offices: Harmondsworth, Middlesex, England

First published 1999
1 3 5 7 9 10 8 6 4 2

Text copyright © Margaret Joy, 1999
Illustrations copyright © Ann Kronheimer, 1999
All rights reserved

The moral right of the author and illustrator has been asserted

Printed in Hong Kong by Midas Printing Ltd

British Library Cataloguing in Publication Data
A CIP catalogue record for this book is available from the British Library

ISBN 0–141–30064–7

Chapter One

Mum was knitting something with white wool.

"I don't want a white jumper," said Addy, "I'd like orange and blue stripes."

"It's not for you this time," said Mum, "it's for our baby. We're going to have a new baby soon."

Addy's eyes opened wide.

"A new baby?" she asked.

"Yes," said Mum.

"When?" asked Addy.

"In a few weeks," said Mum.

"Why can't we have it today?" demanded Addy.

"Because it's not big enough yet," said Mum.

"Where is it then?" asked Addy.

"Here," said Mum, patting her tummy. "It's safe in here. It'll stay here till it's ready."

Addy squatted down and looked hard at Mum's tummy. She put out a hand and felt it.

"Yes," she nodded, "there is a bit of a bump there. Is it a boy baby or a girl baby?"

"I don't know yet," said Mum.
"We'll have to wait till it's born. But
we can have some names ready.
You can help me think of some.
Dad likes John for a boy or Mary
for a girl."

Addy made a face.

"Naah," she said, "there's more
interesting names than that."

She took hold of her plaits, one
in each hand. Then she screwed up
her face as she always did when she
was thinking hard.

"How about . . . um . . .
Cinderella for a girl or . . . er . . .
Pinocchio for a boy?"

"Mmm," said Mum, "we don't
have to make up our minds yet."

"Will it play with me?" asked Addy.

"When it's bigger," nodded Mum.

"What will it be like to start with then?" asked Addy.

"Well, it will be very little, and it'll cry, and drink milk, and fill its nappy and sleep a lot."

Addy looked disgusted.

"That's not much fun," she said, and scowled. "I don't think I want a baby after all. Send it back."

"You can't do that," said Mum. "Wait till it's born, you'll like it then."

Addy scowled again.

"No I won't," she said. She stamped her foot.

"I don't want a baby. I want an orange and blue stripy jumper."

She went out of the room and slammed the door.

"*Huh!*" said Addy.

Chapter Two

Mum always came to meet
Addy after school. She used
to give Addy a big hug and ask her
about her day.

But now she gave Addy a big
hug – and then she talked to Kath's
mum about the new baby.

Addy and Kath always ran on ahead.

"I think you're dead lucky," said Kath, "I've only got two big brothers. I wish I could have a new baby."

"But they're always talking about it," said Addy. "They're not interested in me any more."

"Course they are," said Kath. "What are you going to call it?"

"Oh, I don't know," shrugged Addy. "Perhaps Goldilocks if it's a girl, or . . . er . . . Aladdin if it's a boy – but I'm fed up with everyone talking about this baby all the time."

She ran ahead of Kath and the two mothers. Then she took hold of her two plaits and walked along with her face screwed up, thinking hard.

"I'm going to be bad again," she said to herself. "I'm going to be Addy the Baddy, so they pay attention to *me*. I'll start when I get home . . ."

She ran into the house, looking for something bad to do. First she pulled Tinker's tail so that he screeched and raced upstairs, miaowing, to hide in the wardrobe.

Then she went to the window sill

and picked up a bottle of baby oil,
a bag of cotton-wool balls, a tin of
talcum powder and a huge pack of
nappies. She took them all to the
cupboard under the stairs and
stuffed them in as far as she could.
Then she sat down and looked at a
book and pretended to be reading.

When Mum came in, she looked round and said, "Oh, Addy, what a lovely surprise – you've made everything so tidy!"

"*Huh!*" scowled Addy.

She went out of the room and slammed the door. That didn't work – she would have to think of something else to be really bad.

··· Chapter Three ···

The next day her mum said, "The baby will be born in a few days, Addy. Isn't that exciting!"

Addy took no notice and demanded, "Can we go swimming after school?"

Her mother held her tummy with both hands. The Bump looked

enormous. "I'm sorry, Addy," she said, "I'm really too tired. After the baby comes I will."

"That's no good," scowled Addy, "I want to go today."

She stamped her foot and pulled Tinker's tail again.

On the way to school she wouldn't talk to her mum, and

made horrible faces all the way.

In school she broke Bobby's Lego model of a lighthouse. She put her tongue out at Kevin. She splashed water from the water tray all over Paula's shoes.

She turned her writing book the wrong way up, so that her writing was at the back and upside down.

She squished all the plasticine
together, so that the bright colours
disappeared and all that was left
was a big muddy brown ball.

Then she went into the Wendy

house where Julie was pretending to have a tummy ache. Addy sat on Julie's tummy and bounced up and down, so that Julie shouted out loud, and she *really* had a tummy ache. Miss Mackie told Julie to sit on a cushion in the reading corner till it felt better.

"Addy!" frowned Miss Mackie. "You're being really bad today."

Addy pouted at her, but she was hiding a little secret smile. She was thinking: Good! I'm being Addy the Baddy again. Now what else bad can I do?

She had her next idea at story time. Miss Mackie told them the story of Dick Whittington. He ran away from home with only his cat for company. In the picture in the book he was carrying a bundle tied on a stick over his shoulder. The bundle was wrapped in a red and white spotty cloth.

That's what I'll do, thought Addy. I'll run away from home. Then they'll stop talking about the baby all the time and want me back.

··· Chapter Four ···

When they got home from
school, Mum went and lay
down. Addy fetched her red and
white spotty bathing costume. It
was exactly like Dick Whittington's
bundle in the picture.

Addy laid it out on the bed. She
wondered what people needed when

they ran away from home.

She looked into the bathroom and picked up a box of plasters.

"In case I get blisters from walking a long way," she said to herself.

Then she looked round the kitchen. She picked up a piece of

cheese and an apple and two
chocolate biscuits.

"They're in case I get hungry,"
she said. "That should be enough."

She laid all the things on top of
the bathing costume. Then she tied
the bottom and the straps together
and pulled it tight. It made a lumpy

round bundle, just like the one in the
story book.

She went outside and found a
stick from the garden and pulled it
through the middle of the bundle.

"I'm ready," she said. "Now for
the cat. Tinker," she called, "come
on, Tinker, good puss, come on . . ."

But Tinker was lying on a sunny patch of carpet, fast asleep.

"Come on, Tink," said Addy, and pushed him with her toe.

Tinker looked up at her and hissed. He thought his tail was going to be pulled again.

"Come on, Tink," said Addy.

"We're going to run away together.
Come on, quick, while Mum's
asleep."

She pushed Tinker again with her
foot. The cat shot out a paw and
clawed her ankle.

"Aaagh!" yelled Addy, hopping
round on one foot. "Right then,
stupid cat – I'll go without you."

··· Chapter Five ···

A ddy lifted the stick over her
shoulder and began to walk
away from her house, which was
number 1 The Crescent. She passed
number 2 and number 3.

Then at number 4 she saw
Andrew on the lawn with his
mouse's cage.

He called, "Hi, Addy, what are you doing?"

"I'm running away because we're going to have a new baby," she said, "and they're not interested in me any more."

"Oh," said Andrew. "Well, just stop a minute and help me find Twitcher. He escaped from his cage when I was cleaning it. He's somewhere here under the flowers."

Addy knew Twitcher, Andrew's mouse. She stepped on to Andrew's lawn. They lowered themselves on to their tummies and peered under the plants. There was no sign of Twitcher.

"Twitcher, Twitcher," called Andrew softly.

"We need to make him come out," said Addy. She sat up and undid her bundle. "Here," she said. "Here's a bit of cheese. Sprinkle some little scraps on the edge of the flower bed."

Andrew broke the cheese into bits and scattered them about. Then he and Addy lay down again and waited and watched, very quietly.

Suddenly, a little grey pointed nose, then two pink ears, then some twitchy whiskers, poked out from under the leaves. They held their breath as Twitcher crept out and began to nibble the cheese.

Very slowly Andrew put out a hand and grabbed him.

"Got you!" he exclaimed.

"You're going back in your cage. Thanks, Addy. You can bring the new baby to see Twitcher if you like."

"*Huh!*" said Addy, putting her bundle and stick back on her shoulder.

Chapter Six

A ddy carried on walking.
Between number 5 and
number 6 The Crescent was a strip
of field where an old horse grazed.
She was called Bessie, and Addy
always spoke to her when she
passed by.

Today's Bessie's brown nose was

poking right over the fence.

"Hi, Bessie," said Addy. "I'm
running away – that'll show them."

She stroked the horse's nose until
Bessie threw up her head, neighing,
and shaking her mane.

"I've got something for you,
Bessie," said Addy.

She undid her bundle and took
out the apple. She held it out on the
flat of her hand.

Bessie's big lips gently closed over
the apple. She moved away with it
in her mouth.

Addy could hear her scrunching
it. She wondered if the new baby
would like to see Bessie too.

Addy put her stick back over
her shoulder and went on walking.

She went past number 6, number 7
and number 8 The Crescent.

Suddenly, out of the gate of
number 9 shot little Billy Brown on
his trike. Addy leaped back.

"Watch it!" she shouted.

Billy saw her and swerved, but it
was too late. He swerved so fast
that the trike tipped over.

There was a crash and Billy shot off on to the ground with the trike on top of him.

Addy threw down her bundle and rushed to help him.

"Wah-ah-wah – ow, ow, ow!" yelled Billy.

Both his knees were grazed, but luckily there wasn't too much blood.

Addy put her arm round him and helped him to sit on the edge of the kerb.

"I'll see to it," she said.

She turned to undo her bundle. Billy's crying slowed down and he just hiccuped once or twice as he watched her.

Addy found the plasters.

There were four in the box and she pulled out two of them.

She peeled off the backing and gently pressed one on to each of Billy's red knees. She took out the other two and pressed them on to Billy's grazed hands.

"There," she said. She remembered what her mum had always said and added, "You'll live."

Billy was looking at the plasters.

"They've got dinosaurs on," he said. "Great!"

"You can have the empty box,"
said Addy. "That's got pictures on
too."

She stood up and picked up her
bundle again.

"Where are you going now?"
asked Billy.

"I'm running away because we're
going to have a new baby," she
said, "and they're not interested in
me any more."

"I bet they are," said Billy, "and you'd be good at looking after it."

"Oh, do you really think so?" asked Addy. She smiled – then remembered that she was being bad, and stopped smiling.

"You can bring the baby here, if

you like," said Billy. "We could give it a ride on my trike."

"Mmm, well, maybe," answered Addy and went on round The Crescent.

Chapter Seven

Addy passed number 10, number 11 and number 12. Then outside number 13 she stopped.

A big girl with long fair hair was playing two-ball against a garage wall. She was throwing up the balls and catching them again really fast. Thud-thud, thud-thud, thud-thud,

they were bouncing against the wall.
Addy stood and watched her for a
minute.

Then one of the balls dropped
and bounced away, then the other.

"That was thirty-one two-balls

without stopping," said the girl.

"Wow!" said Addy. "That's very
good. I wish I could do that." She
put down her bundle.

"Where are you going?" asked
the girl.

"I'm running away because we're going to have a new baby," said Addy, "and they're not interested in me any more."

"Course they are," said the big girl. "*I'd* like you for a sister."

Addy's face lit up.

"Would you really?" she said. She opened her bundle. "You can have a chocolate biscuit, if you like," she offered.

They munched together for a little while. Then the girl said, "My name's Charlotte – but they call me Lottie. What's yours?"

"Adelaide," said Addy, "but they call me Addy."

The girl laughed. "That's a great name," she said.

"Do some more two-ball," suggested Addy. "I like watching."

Lottie picked up the balls. Thud-thud, thud-thud, thud-thud.

Suddenly one of the balls went up
too high and landed in the gutter of
the garage.

"Oh, *spit*," said Lottie. "Now I'll
have to wait for someone to get the
stepladder."

"You can try and poke it out
with my stick," said Addy.

She pulled the stick from her
bundle. Lottie took it and stood on
tiptoe, but she couldn't reach the
ball.

"Stand on the dustbin," suggested
Addy.

They pulled the dustbin close to
the garage wall. Lottie scrambled up

on to it. She poked in the gutter
with the stick, but she still couldn't
dislodge the ball.

"I could do it," said Addy. "Stay there and I'll come up with you."

Lottie pulled her up on to the dustbin next to her. Then she lifted Addy high up in her arms.

Now Addy could see over the top of the gutter. She took the stick and gave the ball a hard shove.

It shot out of the gutter in a shower of mud and dead leaves, and bounced down on to the ground.

"Hurray!" they cheered, jumping down off the dustbin.

"Thanks very much," said Lottie.

"That's all right," said Addy. "You can keep the stick in case you need it again."

"OK," said Lottie, "but bring your new baby to see me. We could

take it for a walk. I like pushing
prams."

"Oh, do you?" said Addy in a
surprised voice. She hadn't thought
of that. "OK. Bye, then."

··· Chapter Eight ···

Addy picked up her bundle. It was empty now, so she swung her red and white spotty bathing costume from her hand.

She skipped on round The Crescent, past number 14, number 15 and number 16. Then she realized that she'd come all round The

Crescent. She was almost back
where she started from.

There was her own house again,
just across the road. And her dad
was standing by the gate waiting for
her.

"Hi, Addy," he said. "I've been looking all over for you. Mum said you wanted to go swimming, so I'll take you. Where have you been?"

"Oh," said Addy vaguely, "I just went for a walk around The Crescent . . . but I've got my costume with me already."

"Great," said Dad, "I've got the towels. Let's go."

Two days later, the baby was born. It was a little boy.

Mum brought him home from the hospital wrapped in a white shawl. She sat down on the settee and opened the shawl for Addy to look.

Inside was a baby with lots of spiky hair and a wrinkly red face.

His eyes were tight shut, but one
little hand was poking out, its
fingers moving gently.

"Look!" exclaimed Addy. "He's
waving at me!"

The baby suddenly opened his
eyes. They were bright blue and
they stared straight at Addy.

"Hello, baby," she whispered, "I'm Addy."

Mum said, "This is Billy."

"Billy?" said Addy in surprise. Her eyes lit up. "That's a really good name. Do you think he'll ride a trike?"

"I bet he will," said Mum. "You

can show him how to do it. He's a
lucky boy to have a big sister like
you."

"Yes," said Addy. "There are
loads of things I want to show him.
He won't think I'm Addy the
Baddy, will he? He'll think I'm
Addy the Greatest."